The Snow Wolf

Written by
Maggie Freeman

Illustrated by
Brian Fitzgerald

Ransom

"You can stay with your dad this weekend,"
said Mum.
"OK," said Jack.

After school on Friday, Jack took the bus to the
town where Dad lived. He felt lonely travelling on
his own.

Jack's dad was waiting for him at the bus stop. "Hi, Jack," he said. "Good to see you. Hop in the van. I've one more job to do, then we'll pick up a pizza for supper."
"Your tool box is on my seat," said Jack.
"Oh, I forgot," said Dad. "Stick it in the back."
Then Jack got in the front beside his dad.

"It's quite a way," said Dad. "It'll take us half an hour to get there."
He put on the sat nav and drove out of town.

Soon they were in the country. The van headlights cut into the dark.
"I'm cold," Jack said. He shivered.
Dad turned a knob. "Is that better?" he asked.
"Thanks, Dad."
"The forecast says it'll be minus two tonight."
"It's misty," said Jack.

Jack stared through the windscreen.
They were driving along the bottom of a long valley.
There were no streetlights and no house lights.
Just the moon peeping over the top of a hill.

"Nearly there," said Dad. Then he turned left, and in front of them was a house, with its lights blazing.

"Thank you so much for coming," said the woman at the door. "The boiler isn't working and we're so cold."
"I'll have it fixed in a jiff," said Dad. He took his tool box and went in to the house.

Jack didn't want to go in the house. He stayed in the yard. He pulled his hat down over his ears to keep them warm.

The moon was up now, fat and round and full. Clouds blew part way across the moon. Owls were hooting in the trees – *twit twoo, twit twoo*. It was a scary sound.

Jack thought he saw a white dog trotting
across a field.
"No," he whispered. "No, it's not a dog. It's a …
is it a *wolf*?"
No wolves ran wild in this land, he knew.
But the creature's body was as long as a wolf's.
It was as big as a wolf and as white as snow.
And snow was falling all around it in big flakes.

The snow wolf stopped to look back at Jack. Its eyes were orange. They burned as hot and as bright as candle flames.

"Come with me," they seemed to say.

No way, thought Jack.

So how was it that he found himself running after the snow wolf?

On and on he ran, into the falling snow, though he didn't want to. On and on, until the house behind him was invisible.

He tried to turn back, but he couldn't. Some magic had taken hold of his feet.

On and on he ran, following the snow wolf's
footprints that blazed like fire.
Through trees. Up a steep hillside.
The snow wolf disappeared into a black crack
in a cliff.
I won't fit in there, Jack thought.
Then he thought, *I'll fit if I take this off.*
He undid his jacket zip.
I'll freeze if I take my jacket off, Jack thought.

Clouds slid across the moon.
How dark the night was.
How thick the snow was falling.
He couldn't see the lights of the house in the valley.
He didn't know where he was.
He didn't know where to go.
He was alone, and cold, and afraid.

"Dad!" he shouted into the darkness.
But no answer came.
"Dad!" he called again.
His sad, lonely voice echoed against the rocks.
What could he do?
Jack brushed the snowflakes from his eyelashes.
He saw that where the snow wolf had set its fiery
paws, the snow was still melted. There were dark
prints in the white surface of the snow.
If I follow those prints, Jack thought, *I'll find my way
back to the van.*

He set off down into the silence and the dark of
the valley, following the line of paw-prints.
"Dad!" he kept calling.
He was afraid Dad would have gone home
without him.
"Where are you, Dad? Dad!"
"Jack! Jack!"
That was Dad's voice. "Jack, where are you?"
Suddenly, down there in front of Jack, was the
house in the valley. Its lights shone into the yard, on
to Dad. There was no snow there – the snow had
only fallen up on the hill.

"Dad, I'm here!"
Jack was running.
Dad ran toward him. He threw his arms around
Jack and lifted him up in a great hug, just as he
used to when Jack was a kid, when Dad and Mum
lived together.
"Thank goodness you're safe," Dad said.
"I thought I'd lost you. Come on, let's go. I've fixed
their boiler. Time to get that pizza! Hop in the van."

"It was snowy up on the hill," said Jack. "Funny, there's no snow on the road."

"Sometimes it happens like that," said Dad.

But Jack thought, *Maybe the snow wolf brought the snow.*

He stared through the windscreen.

His eyes ached, searching to see the snow wolf again. But there was no sign of it.

"Dad," he said in the end, "I saw a cave when I was up on the hill. Can I go back to explore it?"

"OK," said Dad. "We'll go tomorrow, when it's light."

"It's a narrow cave. You won't fit in," said Jack.

"I'll wait outside," said Dad. "You can go in on your own."

"Have you got a big torch?"

"It's in the back."

I wonder what I will find in the magic snow wolf's cave, thought Jack, as they drove through the dark to look for pizza.